D0936229

CAPPY CARDINAL

Written and Illustrated
by

FRANK O'LEARY

THE STECK COMPANY

PUBLISHERS • AUSTIN, TEXAS

LIBRARY OF CONGRESS
CATALOG CARD NUMBER 60-6777

To Ricky

Cappy Cardinal was on his way to the Bird Fair.
Cappy was a young gray bird. All cardinals
were gray until the day of the Bird Fair that
year.

The Bird Fair lasted only one day each year.
All of the birds of the forest came to it. No
one wanted to miss it because . . .

. . . there were snowcones to eat and songs to
sing. Some birds made speeches. Others played
in the Bird Band.

Everyone always had a good time at the Fair!

8

On his way to the Bird Fair, Cappy suddenly
stopped. What a terrible sight! Thug Coyote
was chasing Lady Dove, and Lady Dove had a
crippled wing!

10

"Cappy!" screamed Lady Dove. "Help my babies! You know where they are!" Then Lady Dove fluttered into the brush. Thug Coyote raced after her.

11

Cappy was frightened. He flew to Lady Dove's
nest. He told her babies to be very quiet.

12

Cappy waited and waited. Lady Dove did not return. Did Thug Coyote catch her?

Then—plink!—a drop of rain splashed on his head.

The rain began to beat down on them.
Cappy gathered the babies under his wings
and tried to keep them dry.

Cappy was miserable. He wanted to cry,
but he didn't. That would frighten Lady Dove's
babies.

Then a voice called out, "Cappy?"

It was Lady Dove at the bottom of the tree!

"Cappy!" she called. "I escaped from Thug Coyote, but I am crippled and cannot get to the nest. Please keep my babies dry."

"Don't worry, Lady Dove," Cappy said. "I will."

Lightning crashed! Thunder rolled! Cappy was cold and shivering, but the babies were asleep.

Finally the rain stopped. The sun came out.
Cappy saw that it was very late. The Bird
Fair must be over!

Cappy gave the babies some berries. Then he flew down to help Lady Dove.

Cappy bandaged Lady Dove's wing.
"You stay here," he said. "I will go for help."

Just then Cappy heard a noise. In a moment
Cappy's father appeared. There were many other
birds with him.

"Where have you been?" Cappy's father asked. "We missed you at the fair. All of these birds with me helped me search for you. We thought you were lost!"

Lady Dove spoke up. "Cappy has done a very brave thing. He saved my babies from drowning during the rain. He also bandaged my crippled wing."

23

Judge Owl stepped forward. "He missed the
Bird Fair to help Lady Dove," he said. "Cappy
is a brave bird. He must be rewarded for such
courage!"

"I do not want a reward," said Cappy. "I did something any bird would do."

"Not *any* bird, Cappy," replied Judge Owl. "We must all think of what your reward should be."

So all of the birds began to think.

"Look! A rainbow!" said Mrs. Robin.
"How beautiful!" said Mr. Blue Jay.
"And it's coming this way!"

The rainbow moved closer and closer. The
red band of the rainbow moved over Cappy
and stopped.

Then the rainbow leaped back into the sky. Cappy was a brilliant red from head to toe!

"What a beautiful red coat!" Cappy's father said. "What a wonderful reward for courage!"

All the other birds agreed.

Judge Owl yelled, "Tomorrow we shall have the Bird Fair again! Cappy will be the guest of honor!"

For the first time in one hundred years, the
Bird Fair was held for *two* days. Cappy was
King of the Fair!

To this day, when you walk through the woods, you will see many bright red cardinals. Each one wears a red coat of courage!

e

Date Due